For
Samantha — the Wilderness
in the spirit 3
BCarter
1/25/15

ISBN 0-932529-55-0

All inquiries to:
OldCastle Publishing
P.O. Box 1193
Escondido, CA 92033
(760) 489-0336
Fax: (760) 747-1198

Text © A.B. Curtiss 1997
Illustrations © Jules Nathan 1997
Printed in Hong Kong   Library bound on acid-free paper

First Edition 10 9 8 7 6 5 4 3 2 1

Curtiss, Arline B.
 Time of the Wild/A.B. Curtiss
 p. cm.
 Summary: Wild animals teach us
ISBN 0-932529-55-0

1. Wild animals-Juvenile fiction. 2. Wild animals-fiction.
PZ8.3.C8785Ti 1997 {E}-dc20
Library of Congress Catalog Card Number: 97-67224

To my son Ford, also known as Neha, who always knew about trees.   A.B.C.

To my wife, Doris.   J.N.

I suffer from too many roads to take
Too many cities, too much cake.
I'd like to find a spot where weeds still grow.
I'd like to know the wilderness again,
The silence of a tree, the simplicity of snow.
I'm looking for an ancient, honest place
Where they tell time by the clouds.

—CHILDREN OF THE GODS

TIME of the WILD

by A. B. Curtiss   Paintings by Jules Nathan

Long ago there was a time of the wild. It is gone now, except for distant mountains where the flint-eyed eagles fly, or hidden islands where the giant turtles leave their shells. Here lie the dark and misty caves we have not found. Here sleep the animals we have not tamed. Here the Wilderness calls us again and our story will be told by the lessons that we learn.

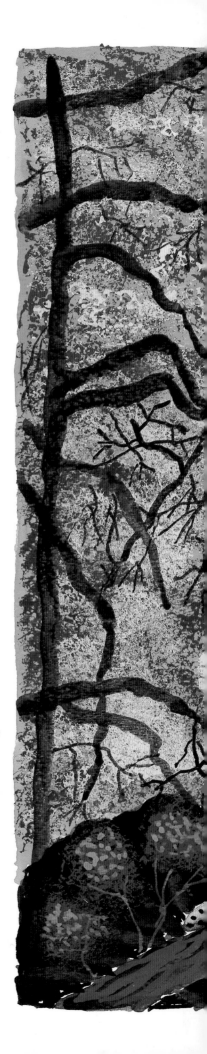

For there is a wisdom in the wildness of things, in creatures that do not live in houses made of windows and doors. There is a strength in flying upon one's own wings. There is a harmony in wearing one's own colors. There is a truth in trusting one's own rootedness so that one cannot easily be plucked from home and set down in a place that one's own father cannot remember.

The Wilderness is a celebration of uncertainty. Trees plant themselves wherever they want, and rivers run down however they please. Mornings are fresh and simple. Sunsets are sudden and bold. Everything is off-hand and first snap; even the day surprises itself. Of course with such perfect freedom, there may be danger anywhere.

B

ut there will also be great comfort in learning under a mother's watchful eye, moving as one in and out of the deep shadows, following behind not too far. This is the calendar of the Wilderness: there is no peace not followed by danger, no danger not followed by peace. This is the salvation of the Wilderness: the emptiness caused by loss in the time of danger is the only space that is available to fill with joy in the time of peace.

I n the wild it is expected that one's real self must be part disguise. This is the creativity of the Wilderness: strange habits and a marked personality. Wilderness never wonders whether one's reality lies beyond these appearances, or if it is these very appearances that form one's colorful reality. This is a Wilderness philosophy lesson: a wise woodland creature simply warns her child, "Take heed, look quick. Oh, the tigers will steal your eyes and you will wonder, are they really there?"

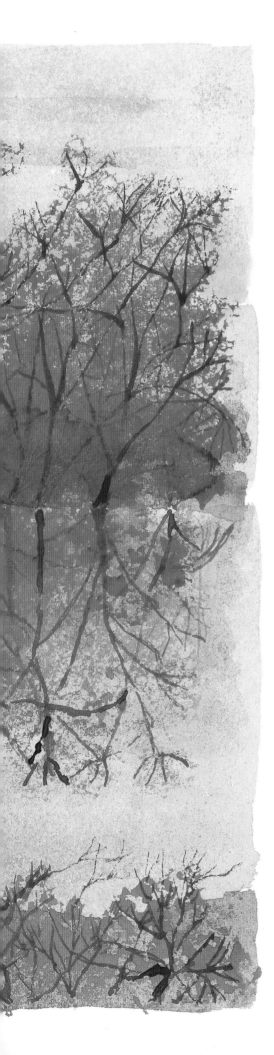

Wilderness never forgets the beauty of the bare essential. Wild birds are as slender and elegant as truth. Their mother is the dance of moonlight on the water, their father is the dark and brooding sand. They exist so sparingly that, when their last times come, they leave behind only the rolling shells and the edges of the night against the shore. This is the wisdom of the Wilderness: grace and silence.

Wild creatures
live so close
to life and
death that
they do not see either one of them
as separate from themselves.
They do not chase time or run
from it. This is the psychology of
wild creatures: each day they rise
new as dawn, and need no
baggage on the trail, for they
carry neither the mistakes of
yesterday nor the hopes of
tomorrow upon their shoulders.
When evening tells them the day
is over, they rest, and do not
struggle to pull back the sun that
has fallen into the sea.

he Wilderness was never a civilized place. Wild creatures have not sailed ships to the moon. They have not built up their security nor learned the freedom of things. But wisdom is more often to be had by bending low than flying high. And there is a dignity in the end of a life whose moment of death serves a fellow creature.

I n the Wilderness there is a music that is born only out of a clean sky. And so the rain washes the thunder. The thunder hurries and complains but the clouds take their own time.

In the wilderness one chatters in a pleasant way about small things. No one cares whether you are right or wrong about something, just that you be easy company for your fellow creature on the path. This is the happiness of the Wilderness: Wild Folk need not remark one another's flaws. Neither do they search for the meaning of life for they are made of it and are never not themselves.

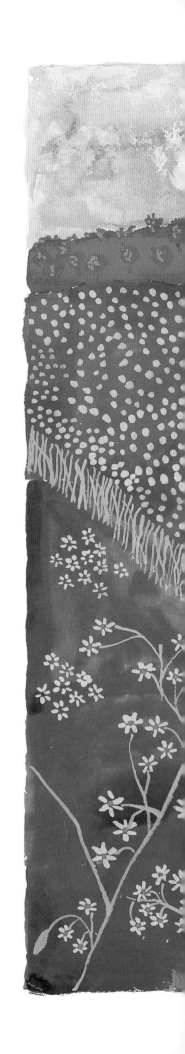

I n the wild there is no safety and nothing is for sure. This is the understanding of the Wilderness: the wonderful terribleness of life. Since nothing can be counted on, no complaint is possible, and thus only gratitude remains. This is the comfort that wild creatures carry for us that we are too young and clever to carry for ourselves.

Oh, there are ancient guardians of the Earth and they reach out to us and wrap our thin hearts in their great silence. In Hawaii the thick arms of the Banyon trees let down their massive tangling of roots into the sand—a living anchor that holds us to the tentative shore. In California the Giant Redwoods rise above us in the most profound majesty of spirit. And how shall we not rise with them?

o understand this one need only walk quietly under the towering trees. Many pass by but the trees have not presumed to mark them. They have borne kindly witness to a million skies. Their compassion is complete. Even birds singing in their branches come to learn from the trees that it is not the bird's own notes but the space between them that is holy. No matter what we might otherwise think, the trees remind us that the only thing we ever really accomplish is ourselves.

Wild creatures are guardians of a great energy that we do not carry for ourselves. There are vast reservoirs of this energy: the mountains, the forests, the oceans, and the deserts. But we are separated from them and do not know how to use them. We are like shells on a shelf that have forgotten the sound of the sea. We are dependent upon wild creatures to help us remember.

The creatures of the Wilderness have long been trying to tell us some immense secret that we have not quite heard. Sometimes we get very close. When we are tired and sad, we look up at the glistening stars, and imagine that they might be looking back at us. When we are frightened and lonely, the trees in the park cheer us somehow. We can be running fast on a hard road when suddenly we catch sight of some small wild thing in our path. We stop and look. We rest a moment. We almost understand.